Forever My Jane

Jungle Island, Volume 2

Sheri Fredricks

Published by Sheri Fredricks, 2016.

FOREVER MY JANE

First edition. October 2, 2016.

ISBN: 979-8231216826

Written by Sheri Fredricks.

Also by Sheri Fredricks

Jungle Island
Lord of the Jungle
Forever My Jane
Jungle Love

The Centaurs
Remedy Maker
Portals of Oz
Troll-y Yours

The Facility
Esme, Door 1

The Rugged Series
Rugged Thirst

Standalone
Monica Beggs
Continuum

Watch for more at https://www.sherifredricks.com.

This book is dedicated to everyone who loves climbing trees, swingin' on a vine, and making mad, passionate monkey love til dawn.

"*Ooh-ooh!*" The gorilla's wide eyes sought them out.

Tarzan hunched down to exchange a flurry of hand and body language with his ape companion, Echo. At the ape's sudden dark expression, he turned towards her.

Jane immediately became alarmed.

Tarzan pointed at the tree. "Jane. Tree."

"What about the tree?" She looked between the two males who remained in their crouched positions, studying the surrounding jungle.

"Up," he replied, the modulation of his no-nonsense voice quieter. "Bad *mans* come."

First survival rule of jungle life: Do as you're told and ask questions later.

Jane grabbed the newly installed vine and with a little of Tarzan's help, she climbed to their sleeping nest.

Only after he had seen that she'd made it to safety, did he and Echo turn and disappear. Between giant ferns and wide-leafed plants, the pair moved as silently as the nighttime shadows.

Any number of bad men could have landed on the island. And what exactly made them *bad*? Maybe they were out fishing and decided to drop anchor for the night.

Maybe, she thoughtfully bit her lip, they were her ticket off the island.

But what about Tarzan? He cared for her deeply, as she cared for him. She might even, possibly, love him. When he left to hunt food, her heart missed him with every beat until a vine swung and he landed back home. How could she ever think of leaving him behind?

An echoing gunshot shattered the air.

Jane jumped, startled in the bed of leaves. Her gaze darted over the edge of her and Tarzan's nest, and then—all the jungle grew quiet.

Chapter One

Damp leaves stuck to the bottoms of Tarzan's feet. His tread light, he ran quickly and ducked behind a growth of leafy bushes. A second *bang* split the moist night air. The sleepy jungle came alive, erupting into the terrified cries of a thousand island creatures. Earlier thoughts of his female's bare butt shattered with the continued rapid pop from the sticks that threw killer rocks.

Human male voices rose in excited babble, calling back and forth, as they carelessly crashed through the plant-filled overgrowth. Birds took to the inky black in a flurry of flapping wings. Small ground animals scattered, rustling underbrush in their haste to race out of danger's way.

The bad mans were not hunters of animals. Even a third year gorilla would know this by the humans' lack of stealth.

Pressed deep into the shadows, across the meandering animal trail, Echo's silver-haired shoulders gleamed in the light of a rising moon. His ape brother stilled as two humans approached.

They passed close enough that Tarzan could reach through the fan of wide-leafed plants and touch their ragged leg coverings.

The armed men walked on, their footfalls heavy and loud from the sturdy feet wraps they wore. As they tramped down the trail, sour body odor hung in the air, then faded away on the evening breeze.

From where he crouched on the ground, Tarzan had a perfect view of the side-to-side movement of Echo's eyes.

His ape brother watched. Waited and sniffed. Took in everything and missed nothing. The ape's gaze swiveled between the disappearing bad *mans*, then landed on Tarzan.

The jungle settled in eerie silence, as if the creatures held their breaths, waiting on the outcome of their unwanted guests. Within a rock throw's distance, the tree he and Jane shared stood silhouetted against a black sky, sparkling like raindrops caught in a spider's web. Above the rim of the sleeping nest, a round object with long hair bobbed, then ducked down again.

As long as his female stayed out of view in the top branches, she would remain safe. A growl rumbled within his chest. He would do whatever it took to keep Jane from harm.

Tarzan clenched his jaw at the thought of her in any type of pain. She made him both laugh and at times, suck air between his teeth while he watched her learn to survive on the island.

Echo's swaying shoulders caught Tarzan's attention. Restless himself, he understood the primal urge of an alpha male to protect and defend.

Soon, he would join Jane in their sleeping nest and would wrap himself around her tiny, curled form. As of the last half-moon phase, they slept with arms and legs twined around each other, like the traveling vines Jane called ivy.

Sometimes the loud calls of howling monkeys jarred him awake. It was those times when an uneasy tightness settled in his chest, the dream just out of reach from his waking mind. The steady in and out of Jane's snorting sleep breath, a loud sound which kept his gorilla family at a distance, wrapped him in satisfying comfort. Much the same as the soft mat she'd woven and used to cover them both.

If the night air left them chilled, it never lasted long. With a grip on her hip and Jane's butt pushed against his stiffened male tool, their nest would settle into a rhythmic rocking motion. Then he and Jane would add their own howls to the sounds of the nighttime jungle.

At the thought of her whimpered cries during their nightly mating, his male part thickened behind his animal skin cover. As plants were drawn to the sun, Tarzan's heart drew him to Jane. Instinct demanded he go to her, but he fought the urge and the persistent banging against his ribs.

Movement from their canopy nest drew his gaze. He glanced upward in time to see his female lean over the edge and view the ground below. Anger pricked at him in the form of beads of sweat on his upper lip. The crackle of branches stretching beneath her movement would draw unwanted attention. While she taught him how to communicate with her mouth sounds, he showed her how to survive in the jungle. They had started with the basics, as if she were an infant gorilla, and she had been quick to learn.

However, the first rule of survival-do as you are told-was not always followed by his too curious mate.

A twig snapped in the opposite direction of where the bad *mans* had gone. Could be an animal searching for food, or it might have been other humans.

Tarzan's gaze cut to the source of sound, his sweaty palm reaching for the hatchet strapped to his thigh. Holding his breath, he stared at a wide shiny leaf as he focused, sifting through sounds; birds distant and near, the soft patter of light rain on plants, the constant drone of insects.

Echo shuffled his feet and broke Tarzan's concentration. Irritated, he cast a brief glimpse across the trail to see the ape adjust his weight with a grunt. Antsy to leave and check the safety of their gorilla band, his brother rocked back and forth with unease.

"*Ooh.*" He tossed a small rock and hit Echo in the arm.

When his brother glanced over, Tarzan lowered his brows and bounced on the balls of his feet. These were the same humans who had hunted Jane a full moon cycle ago. The sight of them had frightened her.

They were bad *mans*, she had told him. They carried guns, a type of rock throwing stick that savagely tore through flesh. Ended life.

Echo shook his massive head. Silvery hair on his sloped crown waved with the motion. His ape brother replied with a deep chest rumble, defying Tarzan's insistence they remain crouched and hidden. His jungle-raised gorilla family would stay out of sight and keep safe.

The cold rain fell in larger drops to splash on his bare shoulders and run down his back. Jane would be out of reach, high in the tree. When the humans did not find what they sought, they would leave the island and never come back.

But if they hurt anyone... *They would never leave alive.*

Ignoring Tarzan's gestures, the great silverback rose from his hiding place and cautiously emerged onto the trail.

"*Ooh!*" Tarzan slapped the ground with an open hand, splashing water collected on the strewn leaves.

Birds squawked back and forth in high branches, their shrill cries widened Echo's eyes and he hunched lower to the ground. Every few steps his knuckles rapped the ground, displaying his nervousness at being vulnerable on the open path.

An ear-piercing boom caused Echo to jump in surprise. Splintering from the direction of the male humans, two more sharp cracks followed closely behind. The immediate wailing cry of an injured animal raised the hair on Tarzan's arms.

"*Ooh-ah-ah!*" Echo lunged forward in a whirl of silvery shadows. He flew down the colorless trail with the speed of a gorilla half his seasons, running as fast as his feet and knuckles would carry him.

"*Ooh!*" Tarzan's warning shout went unheeded.

When it came to bravery, few in the jungle compared to his ape brother. Still, Echo lacked understanding of the power held in the human's long sticks. Tarzan hadn't understood at first either, but Jane showed him the ugly results; round holes in shredded tree bark. Echo would be careful, but fear for their family band could make the great ape careless.

Slowly, Tarzan straightened his legs and directed his ears to the sounds of night. Staring at the shrouded trail, he mentally traveled the route. The path would take the bad *mans* away from the gorilla band and eventually toward the flowing mountain water. Outsider apes and smaller monkeys lived in the surrounding hills, but Tarzan's concern returned to his mate. He would check on Jane first. Only then would he move on to the rest of his family.

One of the jungle's many high-reaching trees stood majestically rooted a short distance away. His fists pounded the ground several times in a four-beat knuckle-lope before he straightened to run on two feet. Chilled raindrops hit his face, his soggy hair hung dripping at his neck. At least the stinging biter bugs had disappeared for the moment.

The trunk of the massive tree spread as wide as Tarzan stood tall. As a youngster, he would have avoided trees such as this. He would have been teased by others in the troop for his inability to make the climb.

That was then, however.

In the *now*, Tarzan stood taller. Ran faster than the rest and swung through the trees better than any in his band.

Today, he stood as a powerful dominant male with a female to mate and protect.

Long strips of bark peeled down from the tree to make temporary non-slip foot and hand holds as he quickly climbed. At the first thick extending branch, he stopped in a crouch to catch his breath. Raindrops lessened and the noise of the jungle increased.

Since the sun's disappearance, only a small slice of moon offered light in which to see. Squinting through the renewed, insect buzzing air, he searched for a single object.

There!

Tarzan directed his feet outward as he stood on the thick branch, curling his back to stay low for balance, then darted forward. The sway of the tree limb increased the farther out he ventured, finally disturbing a group of yellow-beaked birds. They flapped away into the darkness on noisy wings, setting off other birds to squawk in alarm.

The vine lay like a long green snake just out of reach. It stretched from somewhere high in the canopy, to end dangling about chest high. From what he could see in the dark, the trailing plant didn't appear as thick as he would normally choose.

Not far in the distance, the human males shouted their mouth-sounds. Rapid, ugly words he didn't understand. If he stayed on the barren branch, he would risk being seen.

Plants snapped as footfalls plowed closer through the underbrush.

Tarzan wiped his damp hands on the animal hide covering his male tool. Growing up, he had watched others in the gorilla band find warmth and satisfaction with their chosen. Never expecting the same for himself, then it suddenly occurred to him that he had waited all his life for a mate of his own species. His chatty little female filled his chest with fist pounding urges only she could fulfill.

Heart in his throat and Jane on his mind, Tarzan bent his legs and leapt for the skinny vine.

THE INVADERS HAD DEFINITELY not landed for a rescue mission.

"Oh, shit." Jane kept a firm grip on the nest's twig railing while she cautiously peered over the edge. "Where are you, Tarzan?"

What she wouldn't give for a gun of her own.

And maybe a slug of whiskey.

The nighttime sleep platform was more of a crow's nest with woven sides that curled up and a hanging vine which dangled six feet off the ground. Below the precarious structure, the near black jungle lay in steamy bumps and odd shapes. Without the use of a search light, deciphering one object from the next would be impossible.

Two gunshots rang out, followed quickly by a third. Somewhere an animal screamed a gut-wrenching wail.

"Fuck, fuck, fuck!" Jane muffled the words behind the palm she pressed to her mouth. The desperate, high-pitched cries clawed at her heart. Then the suffering yelps grew fainter, spread further apart, and soon stopped altogether. Whatever creature had been shot was most likely dead.

Sickened, she scooted away from the nest's edge to kneel in the center, wrapping her arms over her stomach.

Outside of Tarzan—and the pirates who'd stolen, stripped, then sunk her yacht—she'd never seen another human on the island. If a hunting party landed on the island, maybe they would kill, carve, and leave.

If they're here for food, that is.

A cold shiver tiptoed down the length of her spine. Maybe a gorilla was their target. Plenty of poachers in the world, she'd read about it in one of those *Save the Endangered Species* magazines at the dentist office.

Ah, toothpaste...

"No." She wouldn't let her mind wander to the possibility of either poachers or tooth decay. "Stay positive, Jane."

Roosting birds took to the star-studded sky as branches crackled in the thick foliage below. Leaves rustled as an object traveled. Too small for an elephant, too large for a pig. Whatever it was, it strode with purposeful determination through the rainforest.

Hushed voices in deep tones carried to her ears. They spoke a language she didn't understand—but wouldn't forget anytime soon.

Shudders that curled her body into a knee-hugging ball had nothing to do with the cool night air. It'd been a month, and she'd figured the pirates had forgotten about her and the value she held as the only heir to Porter Investments and their lines of luxury cruise ships. Looks like she'd been wrong.

Jane's heartbeat sped while her upper body flushed with sweat. Lots of people spoke with an eastern dialect. Maybe it wasn't them.

But what if it is? Geezus. It can't get any worse, right?

The rain started as a light drizzle, mocking her. In a matter of moments, a downpour began. At least the warm, humid air warded off a chill.

Jinx!

Cue the trade wind breeze. Jane buried her face in her hands.

Pirates toted modern-day rifles. Tarzan carried a spear.

Even Captain Obvious could figure this one out. Without the Professor's coconut bombs from Gilligan's Island, ingenuity for self-defense would be impossible at best.

In the fight or flight world of the jungle, all creatures made a choice. Her jungleman's proactive decision to follow the pirates served as a reminder in which vine-world she now swung.

Team Tarzan.

Jane lay still as a sloth and held her breath, listening to the sounds outside of their leaf bed, straining to hear anything out of place. Monkeys in nearby sycamores chattered as they rustled and moved through the trees. Nesting alpha gorillas beat their chests and huffed a quiet cadence in the distance—a normal lullaby of the jungle.

As swiftly as the rains came, the drops came to a sudden stop.

The men's voices grew steadily distant until the wild swallowed them whole.

Gathering the edge of her wits and shredded courage, Jane pushed to her knees and squinted through the inky blackness below. Shapes of taller trees and the bushy canopy of fronded plants blurred together as indistinct outlines in the dark.

The three hanging vines Tarzan used in order to swing off in different directions lay hooked for use inside the nest, but no way in hell would she use them. Not only did she flunk elementary vine swinging, but a pendulum's death-defying flight at night would be an irrefutable recipe for disaster. There was no doubt in her mind, she'd do a header and splat into the first available tree.

Damn, Tarzan. He made it look so easy—just grab and go.

Tarzan. How long had it been since his big hands palmed her bare ass, propelling her upward to climb the tree alone?

Five minutes, five hours?

Please don't let that touch be my last memory of him.

Jane arched her back to search the stars, hoping enlightenment would shower her with the ability to read constellations and tell the passage of time. Hell, at least give her the power to divine the future.

Yeah, right. She'd have better luck finding a package of designer panties washed up on the beach. Other than spotting the Big Dipper, the bright dots all looked the same.

Tired and anxious, she rubbed the residuals of the rain off her face with both hands, not caring that the stickiness from the berries she'd eaten earlier hadn't washed away.

"Come on, wild man. Where are you?"

Careful to lift her legs, rather than drag them noisily across the carpet of spongy moss and crunchy leaves, she rose to kneel on the uneven interlaced-branch bed. When she'd first arrived on the island, she had hardly slept. Tarzan, on the other hand, could sleep on his back draped over a branch, with his arms and legs dangling off opposite sides. For a good night's rest and peace of mind, she required more assurance than a coiled muscular arm at her waist could offer.

Thus, the newbie safety rail surrounding their *au-natural*, king-size bed.

Jane held tightly to the nest's woven sides and opened her eyes wide to stare down at the all-consuming dark. A nasty thought popped into her head and kicked her heart into overdrive. After her lungs picked up the cue, her breathing sprinted faster.

If a gun blast hits Tarzan, he'll need me.

This very moment, he could be lying somewhere on the jungle floor, in pain and clutching a wound. His blood might be draining out while his life faded away.

Her fingers drummed the nest's wood frame. Indecision and dread taxed her ability to think smart, coherent thoughts.

The volume of insect noise rose to full blast while Howler monkeys screeched with eardrum bursting decibels. Jane rubbed her palms together, then squeezed them one over the other. No way in hell could she live on the cursed island without Tarzan.

Sure as shit, on her first solo vine swing she'd kill herself, or turn over in her sleep and fall to her death.

Worse yet....she'd live.

Isolated.

It'd be her, all alone on an uncharted jungle island. A sob caught in Jane's throat.

Without Tarzan.

Endless nights of sleeping alone. No muscle-bound arms that'd wake her in the middle of night. No smoky brown eyes smoldering into hers as they made tree-shaking, mind-blowing love a hundred feet off the ground.

Never to touch him again. *Taste him....*

Thoughts of enduring a forced solitude, with only Echo and the other gorillas to keep her company, horrified Jane more than blood-thirsty pirates, swinging on vines, or even the hand-sized hairy spiders that seemed to be every-*fucking*-where.

Warm, humid air ruffled her soggy bangs as she stood. Life without Tarzan was not acceptable. If she cowered in the nest and did nothing, then she deserved nothing in return.

Jane rubbed the back of her neck and made a quick decision. Heart pounding, she reached for the vine that routed her the quickest drop to ground floor level. Butterflies in her stomach swarmed like springtime gnats. Moisture in her mouth seemed to have drained to her hands. She rubbed a sweaty palm over her bare thigh.

An easy slide down the vine, that's all it would take. She'd done it numerous times.

Except never at night and never without Tarzan.

"And never while pirates roamed the island with guns and bullets." *Shit!*

Terrified, Jane hugged the arm-thick vine closer. Gripping the plant in both clammy hands, she eased her trembling legs over the ledge and swallowed her scream.

Chapter Two

Steamy night air slid into Tarzan's lungs with each shallow breath. Humidity dampened the slick, moss covered rocks and the back of his neck. Moisture gathered in the curled leaves at the top of the canopy, filled to overflowing, then plummeted downward to pool in larger leaves. He tipped a stem with his finger and swept the giant drops onto his tongue to quench his thirst.

Other than using his hair, which Jane recently trimmed, he had nothing on which to dry his hands. *Another reason to have long hair.* He leaned his head to the side and grabbed a fistful of shortened strands. Pressing the tangled clump between his palms, he briskly rubbed.

Swinging on a skinny, untested vine was as crazy an idea as Echo swimming underwater. His hairy brother nearly drowned in the lagoon the one time he'd tried, and surely would have if Tarzan had not jumped in and pulled him to shore.

Yet Echo survived, and so would he.

Tarzan straightened his shoulders and took a moment to stare across the blurred distance at the shadowy landing branch. Both arms reaching out in front of him, he took several deep breaths to steady his nerves, swung his arms back and then forward, and pushed off with a fierce lunge, taking his leap of faith. The moment his toes left the branch, his fate became sealed.

Years of experience reflexively curled his hands into constricted balls the moment the damp, thin vine met his palm. Momentum carried him forward, swinging him toward his intended goal. The wind ruffled his damp hair and cooled his heated skin.

Mid-air, the vine gave a shuddering bounce. His grappled hold slipped. Tarzan squeezed both fists, fighting the collected moisture, but he couldn't keep a tight grip on such a scraggy vine. The downward slip skipped in evenly paced maddening jolts. Furiously searching for the tail end with his thrashing legs, his harsh movements only worked to slide him further down.

"Ooh-ooh!" A heavily-laden Acai bough hurtled past, slapping his face with fat purple berries. The impact jarred his movement and threw him off course. Lopsided, his swing turned sideways as he flew toward his final destination.

Another cruel jolt and he slipped a little farther down, the skinny vine slapping his legs as if it were a striking snake. Secured in his position, he tightened his hold, wondering with a sick gut if he had already slipped too far down to make the branch.

Only seconds left to make a decision.

With the vine's short length, the final upward swing would test the reaches of his skill. In order to land safely, he would have to kick hard, let go, and jump the bridging distance.

In the dark.

On a skinny vine.

With damp hands.

Good thing Echo wasn't around to bear a grinning, toothy witness. The gorilla would have had a great time watching the outcome of Tarzan's swinging by a stick.

Sweat broke out anew on his forehead. Jitters of undershooting the tree ran unchecked, as if a thousand dragonflies fought to escape from within. He would only get one chance, and should he miss his landing… Would Jane or Echo find his broken body lying on the jungle floor before the island scavengers nibbled his flesh?

He held his breath. At the precise moment, when both heels rose higher than his head, Tarzan opened his hands and flew feet first like a spear through the air.

"*Ahh-yahyahyah-yah-ahh!*"

An outline of the tree reached toward the sky, its trunk-thick branch shadowed from starlight. The air hung hot and heavy. With a thud that bashed the bones in his spine, he landed with only one foot on the gnarled bark platform. The other foot slipped and shot out behind him.

Wheeling his arms, he immediately sank into a crouched position and dug his fingers into the branch. A relieved huff turned into air sucked between his teeth. The bark scraped angrily on his shin as he pulled up his leg to help balance his squatting position.

Shaken at the narrow escape, he glanced over the side to judge the distance to the ground.

An explosion of angry chatter erupted. He winced after the hours spent sifting through the slightest jungle sounds. Swiveling his head to track the noise, screeches from the white-faced monkey who sat farther along the branch pierced Tarzan's hypersensitive ears.

He tried to soothe the upset beast by offering the back of his hand. "*Ooh.*"

Initially, there had been many lessons for his female to learn in regard to the necessity of quiet. He missed those times. Some days, the only way he could plug her mouth sounds had been to occupy it with something else. Thoughts of Jane's talented tongue thickened his mating tool.

"*Cheep-eep-eep.*" The monkey would not understand silence, just as Jane did not when she first washed ashore.

Should the ear-blasting calls draw the bad *mans'* eyes upward, they would continue to watch the overhead branches. Besides he and Jane, the survival of many animals depended on the jungle canopy for safety.

Shiny black eyes stared back without blinking before the flea-bitten creature threw half an uneaten banana at Tarzan's head.

He dodged easily with an ear tilt toward his shoulder, then caught the flying fruit by its slimy peel before it fell to the ground.

Larger monkeys called warnings in the distance. Ahead, a crisscrossed shield of thin branches prevented him from swinging a direct route to Jane. In the opposite direction, fragrant flowers climbed thorny green creepers that wrapped moss-covered tree limbs. Most certainly a blocked route, unless he wanted his skin shredded.

Frustrated, he slapped the branch beneath the soles of his feet and bounced to shake the tree.

"*Cheep-eep-eep.*"

Tarzan threw the monkey an icy glare. "*Ooh-ooh,*" he muttered, searching for the next vine and an opening to swing. The path didn't have to be safe, just wide enough to squeeze between trees and not hit any rock walls.

Hollow chest beats thumped from afar, followed by a familiar throaty call from Echo. "*Uh-uh-ooh.*"

Tarzan threw a final scowl at the monkey who continued to chatter, then reached for an open vine. With seasons of experience, he would make adjustments and change directions mid-vine if necessary.

Anxious for Jane's safety and knowing her hair-pulling inability to remain quiet, he leapt from the branch and swung for their nest.

The moment he jumped, too late to turn back, a warm coil wrapped his neck. As the wind whistled past his ears, he glimpsed upward to the white-faced monkey who tagged along for a ride. Wide-eyed and open-mouthed, the little animal's hands clung to the vine above Tarzan's head while its choking tail kept him from falling below.

Trees whizzed in a blur as they swung through the air. With the little monkey draped over his head, Tarzan landed on giant limbs of ancient trees, only halting long enough to gather his bearing before vine-skipping through the jungle like a rock across water. Muscles in his upper body screamed from the effort of holding his body's full weight. Warm air blew through the strands of his hair as if massaging his scalp. The monkey chirped its excited cries. Giant leaves and thick branches blended into a fuzzy haze as they picked up speed on the downhill swing. Sweat on Tarzan's forehead dried, his heart thumped in his chest.

Exhilarated by the sense of flying, a grin stretched his lips as he kicked his legs and swung for home. Thoughts of his mate's soft thighs, warm woman's fur, and wet channel created a sense of urgency only hindered by the stomach dropping sensation of the vine.

Almost home. He bit back the jungle cry poised at the end of his tongue.

Between the monkey's crossed arms, Tarzan glimpsed bright dots in the night sky that spread as a backdrop to the dark silhouetted outline of the sleeping nest. Knowing how sudden surprises turned Jane from cooing smiles and a wiggly butt that raised his tool, to lowered brows and a sharp voice even the animals feared, he lifted a hand to bracket his mouth and softly called out to her, "*Ooh-ooh*-Jane."

His deep grunts blended with the other nighttime jungle racket. If she remained alert, as he had taught her, Jane would easily pick out her name as a foreign sound.

"*Chee-chee-tah*." The little monkey added his personal high-pitched chatter, his tail squeezing Tarzan's neck a little tighter.

The shadowed sleeping nest edged closer on the upward swing. On the ground below, stomps of crunching deadfall caught his attention. He swiveled his head toward the sound. A wall of impenetrable black shadow met his eyes. By the amount of rustling, it was probably an animal searching for a meal or location to bed down for the night.

He, too, looked forward to settling in his nest...and covering his female from behind. A thrill shot straight to his tool, one that tingled his male part as it grew.

Tarzan released the grip of one hand to reach up and carefully unwind the short-haired tail that wrapped his neck. Past the lowest midpoint, the vine swung up. He waited until the sleeping platform's curved edge loomed beneath his feet. Then, at the precise moment, he let go of the vine and lightly dropped in a crouched position—inside an *empty* nest.

"*Chee-tah!*" The monkey landed on all fours beside him.

SOMETHING WICKED THIS way flies...

The stupid slightly altered verse looped through Jane's mind while she frantically searched the darkness above for the source of rustling. If it'd been Tarzan, he would have called out to her. Monkeys most likely, she surmised, going by the high-pitched chirpy sounds.

A traipse through the undergrowth after dark didn't sit high on her bucket list, but the thought of never seeing Tarzan again or making crazy monkey-love high in the trees, propelled her toward the direction where she'd heard the injured animal cry out.

Kookaburras called from their obscure roosts, lending their voice to the jungle drama as if she acted in a B-rated horror movie. Jane picked her way along the trail mostly by feel, since the half-moon's meager light shone in splattered patches through the trees. Droopy elephant ear shaped leaves, which provided relief from the sun during the day, worked in the same vein against her at night. Like the vocal equivalent of a rainforest security lighting system, croaking frogs became silent when she drew near. After she passed, the jungle watch-dogs started up again.

Darkness hid landmarks she would have recognized during the day. She pinched her brows and squinted in the low illumination, following the path as it twisted around coconut palms, under fallen trees, and through a swampy bog. When the giant fern with a broken frond seemed all too familiar, she came to an abrupt stop.

"Where the hell am I?" Exasperated, Jane glanced around to find a bearing. The living jungle seemed to replicate itself every few steps.

A loud thump hit the ground back in the direction from which she'd come. Slowly, she turned to look into the dark behind her. No amount of hard staring would cut through the muggy blackness. Leaves swished, brushing a moving object.

An object that moved toward *her*.

A shriek threatened to burst from her throat, but she turned to face forward and fled blindly down the trail. Upraised roots tripped her steps. Sharp rocks bruised the bottoms of her bare feet. Jane chanced a quick glance over her shoulder. In the nonexistent light, everything seemed to meld into one giant blob. If she could just find a suitable tree, she'd reach for a lower branch and climb to safety.

Silken threads of a dew-laced substance fanned lightly over her face.

"Eww!" She used both hands to rapidly brush off her face. Fucking spider webs were everywhere. Arachnids as big as her hand, with spots and bright colors...at the phobic thought, a tremor ran up her spine and shook her shoulders.

"Keep movin', Jane," she mumbled and forced her clumsy feet forward.

Childish fear of enormous eight-legged creatures who clung for a ride spurred Jane to continue slapping at her face and hair. As if in a bad dream, her feet constantly tripped, slowing her pace. Thoughts of other creepy-crawlies underfoot and in the foliage, pressed in from all sides. Regular breathing became gasps.

A tree suddenly loomed up on her right. Crooked, finger-like branches reached out from under the hideous shadows like a dark specter of lore. Jane stumbled, catching herself against the trunk with one hand. A light tickling tap-danced across the back of her knuckles and she yanked back to give her hand a vigorous shake.

Oh God, why did there have to be bugs everywhere?

Over the cadent chirp of crickets, a four-beat rhythm pounded the ground, running fast and drawing closer.

Stretched onto the tips of her toes, she frantically waved her fingers, reaching for a sturdy overhead branch. Exertion burst from her mouth, sawing in and out. No matter how far she extended her arms or if she jumped high, she just couldn't reach the damn branch.

Plant stalks snapped violently to the side behind the feathery fronds of the fern to her right. Jane stepped back from the tree, then panicked as she realized her mistake. Hiding behind the narrow trunk would be a hell of a lot better than getting caught in the open.

With her heart pounding, she leapt forward to take cover behind the tree.

Chapter Three

After he left the monkey, and climbed down from the nest, a bad feeling rolled through and squeezed Tarzan's chest in a tight grip. Unable to breathe, he opened his mouth and gasped for air. The crushing force continued to increase, as if an elephant wrapped him within its strong *nose-arm*. Normal sounds of daily jungle life carried on around him, paying no heed to his discomfort and sense of doom.

Where would she be?

A familiar sweet scent tantalized the moist air. Stretching out in his fast-paced knuckle-lope, he ducked past leaves and dodged branches at skull-cracking heights.

He sniffed again as he hurried along.

Jane.

A heavy shroud of dread grew inside him for her safety. Tarzan tested the limits of his endurance, ignoring the scream of his tired muscles. With a reckless backswing, he knocked a large plant out of his way, leaping over the stalk when it snapped in half. Under normal circumstances, he would have treaded quietly, keeping his presence unknown. However, since his unskilled female wandered alone in the jungle with both night predators and bad *mans* on the hunt, he would risk the chance of discovery.

He shoved past a sapling palm and paused where the trail opened wider. The sight of Jane surrounded by a pool of moonlight, in the open for all to see, nearly stopped the beating of his heart. Had she learned nothing?

She jumped back from a weak-limbed tree she stood beside, then turned to dive behind its skinny trunk. In the bright clearing, she cast an obvious shadow wider than the tree.

Close enough for her to hear, he whispered, hoping to not startle her, "Jane!"

Tarzan gathered his strength, digging the balls of his feet firmly into the damp soil littered with dead leaves. He glanced about for signs of danger before leaping forward, wrapped his arms around her slim body, and took the brunt of the fall on his back.

The whites of her eyes gleamed and were open wide in a terrified mask as the shock of surprise took hold. She let out a squeal and thrashed violently, kicking her legs while twisting back and forth.

"*Ooh-ooh.*" To silence her, he flipped their position and pinned Jane beneath him. When she opened her mouth to make more noise, he pressed his lips to hers.

A lazy moving warmth, like honey straight from the hive, spread outward in a delicious tingle from where their dancing tongues met. Slowly, her rigid muscles relaxed, and he raised his head to gaze into blue eyes ringed with black lashes.

"Tarzan?"

His heart hammered. Resting his forehead against hers, he struggled to breathe and find the right words to convey happiness in finding his female safe. Unable to think of the tones she had taught him, he fell back on what he knew.

"*Ooh-ooh.*"

Tarzan patted Jane's cheek with the back of his hand. Better than any mouth sound, he needed to lay open the secret depths of his heart. He would show her by using his primal ape language. He stared into her sultry eyes, watching how they widened in understanding when he ground his mating tool into the soft flesh of her sex.

In many ways, his female lived her jungle life as that of an infant gorilla—inexperienced in the ways of his world. Feeling the full strength of his proud male part stiffen in need, he would leave Jane no doubt as to his feelings for her.

Alive and well, his mate's hands clung to the trembling muscles along his back. Pressed to her body and inhaling her scent should have been enough to alleviate the fright of having almost lost her.

But it wasn't. He needed more.

Tarzan needed proof through senses that didn't require his eyes or nose. He needed to feel her warmth wrapping his hardened length, to hear her soft groans whisper his name.

Her finger grips changed to stroking when he slanted his lips across hers. His warm, soft mate coiled her shivering arms around his neck and held tight, as if to never let him go.

Reluctantly, he pulled back to stroke the hair out of her eyes and hover a breath's space above the lips he dreamed of day and night. "Jane hurt?"

Night's darkness held the secrets of her eyes, though she stared into his. She shook her head, rattling dead leaves under her hair as her shaky words rushed out. "No, I'm fine. There was gunfire and—I thought you'd been shot."

Other than *No*, he didn't understand all of her sounds with his limited grasp of her language. It didn't matter, she lay safe beneath him now.

An emotion filled him to near bursting, one that took over his body more often since the day he had found her laying half-drowned in the surf. He touched their foreheads together and closed his eyes, reveling in the squeeze of her trembling arms.

"Where were you?" she hissed. "When you didn't come back, I got so worr—"

Tarzan grinned and pressed a quick kiss to her flapping mouth without opening his eyes. Happiness warmed him to have the porcupine side of his female return.

"Yes, I'm glad to see you, too," she huffed. "But you didn't—"

This time when he pressed his lips to hers, Tarzan gave Jane's tongue something to do.

Chatter and more chatter, always moving with the mouth sounds. His female never understood the importance of silence.

IT TOOK MENTAL CALISTHENICS with eyes squeezed shut to remind herself that they lay on the icky jungle floor amongst *God-knows-what* kind of insects. Though, she'd better get used to it because this is where she lived now, as a primitive in a wild jungle. No running water or electricity, no screens to keep the bugs out. Survival reality TV shows were a drop in the bucket compared to this.

Jane skimmed her fingertips along Tarzan's sun-bronzed neck, then stroked the day's growth of stubble covering his strong jaw. She used her tongue to trace his sexy lips and opened her eyes when the sexy wild man lifted his head for a much needed breath of air.

His hooded eyes smoldered as his gaze caressed her face. With his jaw slack and his lips wet, he looked ready to devour her.

The thought of exactly *how* he might dig in and accomplish that naughty task tingled her lips, both top and bottom.

Bugs? Ha! What bugs!

"Tarzan?" Jane inhaled his natural scent of cinnamon and clove. The mix worked like a double-whammy shot of strong bourbon that slid her senses along a drunken path of longing.

"Yes, my Jane?" He plucked her nipple with his lips.

Heat sizzled into her body from his steel-banded arms wrapping her body. The moment he'd lowered his head and took her lips, nature had set its broiler fans on high to blast over her heated skin.

"You feel incredible," she said, sliding her fingers into his hair and combing through his silky shoulder-length tangles to massage the base of his neck. "Your hair is so soft."

"Jane soft, too," he whispered. With a subtle shift of his sculpted thighs, he burrowed tighter against her aching core.

Apparently, it wasn't close enough for his liking because he grunted and slid a hand under her hip to tug her a wasted millimeter closer. His palm didn't remain still for long; it slid lower, cupping the back of her thigh, then he raised her knee high to hook an arm around and keep her leg in place.

Her dampness rubbed against him, coating his stiffness with her ignited passion. Jane shivered, knowing he would recognize the sign of her arousal.

Tarzan's low chuckle rumbled through his chest and pushed her nipples to catch the vibration. His hardened cock, in all its engorged splendor, rubbed the sweet spot craving him most. "Jane safe."

"Yes, I'll always be safe with you, wild jungle man." But who would keep Tarzan safe? He knew next to nothing about the modern ways of life, a fact currently roaming their island this very moment. Pirates carrying loaded guns made education a one-time learning experience.

Thoughts of danger and whether or not they would live to see tomorrow evaporated as he retook possession of her mouth. He'd found her tongue to suck when his rigid cock prodded, then slid inside. The hatchet strapped to his thigh scraped the inside of her leg, a grim reminder of the ongoing jungle island danger.

He didn't waste time and went straight into a hard, marvelous ride.

The moan-inducing pressure found only in Tarzan's arms, rapidly built below. Jane arched her neck, straining, digging into the dirt with her heels and cupping her breasts. She needed his hands. Needed the magic in his fingers to erase all her hours of terrified waiting and the unrevealed terror yet to be.

"Please," she rasped, rotating her hips. "Touch me. I love the way your hands feel on my body."

Nature's night light filtered down through the leaves and reflected on her wild man's wolfish grin. "*Ooh-ooh.*"

Chapter Four

Tarzan's persistent lips worked an enchantment down the side of her neck as his cock drove with sensuous play against her core. Jane opened her thighs wider, needing more of him, and her wetness increased.

They'd been lucky—hell, *she'd* been lucky. If he had been shot, perhaps mortally wounded—Lord, she couldn't let her mind slide into that bleak, dark hole. Not when the comfort of his weight proved him solid and real.

The rapturous onslaught over her throat intensified, she tilted her head and gave him room to work.

"Tarzan," her lover's name came out as a breathy moan in the humid night air. She tightened her arms around his shoulders, squeezing him closer to alleviate the persistent ache of her nipples rubbing his chest hair.

Between her fear for his safety, the phobia of climbing from their nest, followed by a terrifying search of the darkened jungle floor, a stream of volcanic emotion erupted through Jane. The man she loved with all her heart held her in his strong protective arms. Adrenaline surged with every pulse beat, raising the level of her passion.

Tarzan's warm, moist mouth traveled down one side of her throat, then licked and sucked his way up the other as he made hot jungle love to her. With a muffled groan, he settled his lips over hers once again. Insistent, his tongue demanded entry, pressing the seam of her pliant lips until Jane opened on a sigh and gladly invited him in.

Like an alpha gorilla, he charged forward and took control of the fiery crush of their mouths. One of Tarzan's hands fisted in her hair and held her still, a subtle dominant move to remind her that he was lord of the jungle and presided over all.

"Jane taste good," he murmured. His hips pounded a faster rhythm. Each knocking surge shoved at her body, moving her over the ground in increments.

"So do you."

Tarzan's unique flavor tasted of the jungle; a raw, wild power. An essence so intoxicating, she found herself forever hooked as a willing addict. Tingles of exquisite warmth tensed deep within her core.

"God, whatever you do, don't stop." She cried out her passion and gripped his sweat-dampened back. Muscles flexed and coiled beneath her fingers.

From a distance, a call of the apes reverberated through the night air. Birds squawked a sudden burst of chaotic noise, then quieted just as quickly. Hushed sounds of an animated jungle played a melodic background symphony to her ears.

"*Ooh-ooh-ooh.*" Tarzan's powerful thrusts shortened. His pumping hips lurched off-balance. Sliding his hand between their sweat-moistened bodies, his fingers played at the quintessence of their connection.

The Lord of the Jungle continued to hammer away. Sounds of their furious lovemaking—hot, wet, carnal—soothed her frightened soul. She pulled her knees higher, tilting her hips. Grabbing a handful of his hardworking ass in each palm, she urged Tarzan's ramming thickness inside her. Needed the hard strikes of his pelvis against hers more than she wanted a rescue from the island. Desperate for him to fuck his way to completion, to take what belonged to him and leave his evidence behind.

"Oh, God. Yes, Tarzan!" The feather-light pinch to her sensitized clit worked like an atomic bomb to her bliss tormented body.

Jane arched her back and exploded. Her hands fell away to lay beside her head as he straightened his arms to rise above her. Manhandled in the very best way, her loud moans echoed when he sunk his cock to a mind-blowing depth. His eyes closed and his mouth dropped open as his face lifted toward a sky painted with stars.

Tarzan thrust once. Twice. Then threw his hips forward and stiffened. "*Ahh-yahyahyah-yah-ahh!*"

The wildman's cry breached the steamy jungle air like a horn blast from a battlefield soldier.

TARZAN COULDN'T REMEMBER a time when he felt as boneless and relaxed as he did right then. Beneath his well-sated body, with his mating tool rooted deeply within, Jane's soft breasts cushioned his chest as his breathing slowed to normal. Soothed by the scratchy strokes of her fingernails lazing across his back, he closed his eyes and burrowed his nose deeper into the side of her sweet smelling neck. Not even the thought of bad *mans* could rouse a growl out of him.

Somewhere in the distance, a gorilla drummed its chest. By the offbeat pattern, the performer had to be his best friend and ape-brother, Echo. Tree monkeys answered with howls of their own, possibly laughing, but Tarzan didn't speak their shrill language.

Jane's hand paused a moment. "I love you."

"Love?" Tarzan yawned and rolled off his mate. He stretched both tired arms overhead, then grunted as he pulled himself to his feet with the help of the tree.

A blanket of drowsiness drifted over, ready to tuck him in. It would be good to sleep high in the tree while their enemy's eyes stayed open and grew tired. While he didn't understand the meaning of Jane's word, she had used it many times when eating her favorite sweet fruits. The female was always hungry. Did she want a banana from the tree a few strides away?

He sighed. "Jane, no eat. Sleep time in nest—"

A deafening crack split the peaceful night air. The meaty, round part of his shoulder flared with a sudden burn. He slapped a hand over the choking pain as Jane screamed from where she lay on the ground.

"Get down," she shouted, yanking at the animal skin that covered his male part. The thin support string snapped and the hide lay useless in her hand.

Another loud bang, then a high-pitched whine. The grandfather of all biting bugs tore through the leaves. Wood chips flew back at his face from the tree next to his head. He stared in wonder and moved his hand from his bleeding shoulder to stick a finger inside the jagged hole.

"Tarzan!"

Jane's harsh whisper cut his curiosity short. He glanced down as she grabbed the elbow of his uninjured arm, tugging with what seemed her entire body weight, until he crouched beside her on the ground. Plants rattled, the sounds of movement approached.

"Are you hurt?"

Another loud bang, and more splinters rained down on their heads. Sleepy aftereffects of their mating time vanished.

"No." Drowsiness moved out. In its place, anger ignited a raging fire and he gritted his teeth. "Tarzan peed."

"You what?" A crease separated her tightly drawn brows. She stopped examining the burning pain in his shoulder to glance into his face. A moment later, one delicate brow rose in understanding. "You mean you're pissed?"

They dared to walk upon his territory. Threats from death-sticks would not stop Tarzan. He alone stood as the jungle island alpha male, and he had allowed danger to continue for too long. Neither Jane nor the gorilla band would be hurt.

If pain had found any of his family...*Tarzan will kill bad mans.*

Behind the banana tree, a large-leafed bush swayed unnaturally. Shiny black eyes, darker than the night, gleamed from between two fronds in the weak moonlight. "*Ooh.*"

"*Ooh-ooh,*" he answered Echo's inquisitive tone before turning to Jane. He carefully masked the rage building within his chest. "Tarzan stop bad *mans.*"

"No!" Her hand flew up, gripping his arm close to the wound, and he hissed. "You can't go out there. Honey, they'll shoot you."

Love and honey. Why was food always on Jane's mind?

Chapter Five

"Tarzan, wait. Listen to me." Jane darted a gaze at their surroundings, then scrambled to follow.

He turned and threw her a hard stare that stopped her in her tracks. "You're already hurt. They'll leave when they can't find me, just like before."

What she wouldn't do for a neighborhood drug store; clean bandages, orange antiseptic paint, penicillin for him and an aspirin for her. Without a flashlight, she couldn't determine the condition of his injury. The unknown drove her crazy with fear, and she was close to flipping out anyway.

Stubborn jungle man. Going all *Predator* on the pirates would do nothing except get him killed.

She glanced at Echo, the huge silver back gorilla who'd been Tarzan's constant companion from the moment she'd coughed up seawater beachside a scant two months ago. His giant sloped head radiated the moon's glow as he followed their argument back-and-forth.

Tarzan motioned toward her with the back of his hand. "*Ooh-ooh.*"

Echo grunted, apparently agreeing with whatever the ape man said.

"Jane, go to moon bed." He stepped away.

Her heart sank. *Here we go again.*

She raised a hand to cover her mouth, holding back the fear lodged like a chunk of breadfruit in her throat. "No," she begged, shaking her head. "Don't go. Please."

Tarzan hunched over, knuckle-walking his lithe body away from her as he kept to the shadows. At a patch of moonlight, he paused and crouched. His brows were lowered in a fierce scowl as he glanced at her over his shoulder. "Go."

Go? A single word, no kiss goodbye? Not a hug, pat or quickie before he left? She wasn't some child to be sent away. For better or worse, her place was with Tarzan.

Jane twisted her hair into a knot and tucked the end tight to hold. Like it or not, she'd be going with him. He didn't know the first thing about rifles and the impact of a bullet when it hit a human body. Taking a deep, unsteady breath, she copied Tarzan's crouch and took a step forward.

Echo's gigantic arm gently wrapped her waist.

Surprised, she pushed against the soft hair covering his steely band. When he didn't let go, she pushed harder.

It'd would have been easier to push the trunk of a tree.

"Stop it!" Nitwit ape picked the wrong time to play. "Tarzan, will you tell him to let go of me?" Jane struggled and pulled at the long fur covering Echo's arm as he turned them away from her jungle man's brooding eyes. Shouting would only endanger them all, and she refused to draw attention to their location.

Across the darkness, she locked eyes with her silent alpha man. His jaw clenched tight, resolute in his decision. This wasn't his battle to fight. The pirates never would have come if she hadn't drawn them to the island.

"Don't leave—me." Her voice cracked as her fingers reached out into the empty air.

This was all her fault.

Before the jungle removed Tarzan completely from view, he lifted the back of his hand in her direction. "*Ah-ah*. Jane—"

The hanging ivy and giant ferns swung like a natural slamming door to sever their connection.

"Tarzan," she whispered, glancing back over the bulk of Echo's massive shoulder.

The great silver back knuckle-walked one-handed, dragging her along with nonchalant grace. "*Ooh-ooh.*"

Probably the ape's way of saying "Don't worry." But worry she would until the elephants came home, if need be.

Echo led her directly to the bottom of her and Tarzan's sleeping nest, then sat on his haunches and waited. He studied her agitation with big, knowing eyes that stared straight into her soul.

"Will you watch over him?" Stupid of her to try and communicate when the gorilla understood zilch of what she said.

Echo cocked his head and slapped the tree as if he were bored. With an arrogant flip of his hand the Queen of England would envy, he motioned for Jane to start climbing.

For all the different possibilities of Jungle Island *ooh-ooh*, this latest translation had assigned her a bodyguard.

So, Tarzan hadn't said goodbye before he left, then. She'd hoped, but...

The knowledge brought a pinch of sorrow to her chest.

After a final glance into the dense foliage where she could see absolutely nothing, Jane grabbed the vine and hauled her broken-hearted ass up the tree.

THE ISLAND PATHWAYS were laid out with all the logic of a thousand ant trails. Unless the jungle animals traveled the routes often, the creatures would be lost before their second turn.

Tarzan scanned his familiar jungle. Every broken plant stem caught his eye, as well as the scent of over-turned, moss covered rocks.

The comfort of his knuckle walk allowed him to creep low to the ground, the gorilla-style method of travel made tracking the humans that much easier. His ears picked out nothing unusual and his eyes viewed the same. The hatchet's wooden handle on his hip tapped his thigh with every forward movement.

These bad *mans* were either brazen or stupid, leaving a trail an infant could follow. Their destructive path of crushed plants and torn soil curved around trees covered with moss, but at the last downhill pitch before the stream, slick mud atop solid ground turned into a sloppy mess. Toward the streambank, two boulders sat with muddy tops and sides.

The frogs were quiet. Little bush birds too.

Hair rose on the back of his neck as he scrutinized an open stretch of trail where the moon's light shone brighter. The nighttime rainforest air smelled of turned soil and old leaves. Humidity hovered as a moist blanket covered the island.

Cold sludge oozed between his toes, and Tarzan stepped carefully to avoid the path's sloppier sections. Regardless of care, mud slid out over hard-packed ground. His feet slipped faster than he managed to balance. As he shot toward the large rocks at the bottom of the decline, he reached with his hand to grab a passing limb—and came away with a fistful of leaves.

His right foot hit the gravel in the streambank first, which gave him purchase to push away from the rock's sharp edge and slide safely in-between.

Snap! A strong sapling burst forth, popping upright from its bent position. The next moment, *whoosh!* A scratchy net swallowed him whole.

The sensation of being *flung* into the air differed greatly than flying through it. His stomach made a lurch for his throat the same time the ground disappeared beneath his feet.

Stunned at the rapid turn of events, Tarzan lay on his back for a moment inside a bag of thick woven coils. The gentle swing back and forth over the shallow stream might have been relaxing any another day. However, today it held a deceptive edge.

The night sky peeked through the weave as he pulled his scattered thinking parts together. A chill of unease grew in his core. In the opening at the top, the trap gathered in a circular knot. *Too small of a space to squeeze through.*

With the low light, it was impossible to study exactly how the net was held together. He would need to stand. Though, having his feet not fall through the net's open holes while achieving an upright position wasn't easy. Hand over hand he climbed, gaining an upright position one moment, only to have his foot fall through the next.

"*Uh*." Tarzan scrubbed a hand over his two-day growth of bristle. The lack of facial hair, a relatively new feel, scratched against his palm and helped to focus on solving his problem.

Reach, hold, step. Repeat. Finally, when he stood full height with both unsteady feet planted through the holes in the net, Tarzan reached his hand through the top opening to touch the ropes that held the net together. His fingers flew over a tight knot made from more of the same coarse material and gathered a mental image of what he found.

The more he touched, the further his stomach fell. Unfortunately, there would be no springing the trap from within the net.

Plants rustled, followed by rumbled tones of human males speaking low. Still some distance away, but close enough to hasten the beat of his heart.

Tarzan pulled the hatchet from its leather case strapped at his waist. He ignored the wood handle and held it straight at the stone head. Amply sharp to slice through any game caught for dinner and sturdy enough to chop through jungle plants, the first link of rope under his feet still took forever to saw through.

The bad *mans'* harsh language burned his ears. Not at all resembling the soft flow of Jane's mouth sounds. The hatchet cut through the length of rope. He grabbed another section and sawed furiously, lifting his eyes off the task only to glance in the direction of the approaching enemy.

The ache in his injured shoulder tore through his arm. He ignored the blood seeping from the wound and kept hacking away. The fibrous rope split into two, and he immediately set his hatchet to another link. Sweat dripped into his eyes, causing them to sting and water. There would be time to look at his shoulder later, but only if he cut his way out before the bad *mans* arrival.

The stench of unclean bodies drifted in the movement of air. This time when plants rustled, Tarzan also saw the leaves stir in the darkness. Tops of three rounded heads bobbed and snaked closer.

Hurry, for Jane.

Beneath him, the twisted cordage slowly frayed under the hatchet's sawing pressure, one line at a time. Tarzan stomped his foot, breaking the last individual strand and dropped through the opening to land in the water. Crouched near the bank, the icy water swirled around his thighs.

The human males exited the jungle. Tarzan held his hatchet tight and sunk deeper into the stream, the chill catching the breath in his throat. Arms stretched out for balance, he lifted his feet from the pebbled rock bottom and lay back, allowing the current to float him downstream.

Chapter Six

Brilliant hues of orange pierced Jane's sleepy eyes. She lay naked on her back, watching dawn break over the tallest trees, painting the overhead sky all sorts of sickeningly cheery colors. Ignoring the filth that covered her hands, she scrubbed the tear tracks from her cheeks. It'd been hours since Echo led her away from Tarzan. Hours since he'd gone off and—and....

A stuttered inhale shook her chest. God, it hurt. Not only did her heart suffer, but she'd have to endure the pathetic emptiness when she went too long without her wild jungle lover. Just thinking about him brought a needy ache between her thighs.

The tick-tock of her body's clock was a bitch.

Jane clamped her knees together, but that only worked to intensify the torture of his absence. Another sob broke through the gridlock in her throat. The discomfort at her core pulsed with a tantrum to be satisfied.

"Tarzan." She drifted a hand over her stomach and shut her eyes to the ballet of birds above. "Where are you?"

Tears continued to leak from the corners of her eyes. They dripped an itchy path while she combed her fingers through the soft curls between her thighs that'd grown back since washing up on the island. Oh, how excited he'd been to discover her smooth skin down below. How he had knelt between her legs and pushed her thighs wide apart, then leaned down for a closer inspection.

Jane skimmed her fingers past her clit and cupped her wet need, hoping the pressure would alleviate her desperation for Tarzan. Sadly, her hand only stoked the fire within. Faced with sexual tension brought on by her own hand, she accepted her body's demands.

The slide of a finger, a push further in. A few laps around her sensitive nub. Harder, faster, her hand spread the growing wetness. Behind closed eyes, she conjured an image: Tarzan's cock jutting strong and proud as she gazed up at him from a kneeling position. His hand would take a fistful of her hair and guide her mouth to him.

She pinched a tight nipple with her other hand. The taste of him...she moaned just thinking of his masculine flavor.

"*Ooh-ooh.*"

Tarzan? Laying down had worsened the stuffy nose she'd gained from crying. She sat up, sniffing loudly, then moved to peer anxiously over the lip of the nest. While her hand soothingly rubbed the persistent need of her body, she hoped against the odds she would see Tarzan down below.

Who sat in a crouch wasn't her errant lover, but his sidekick banana-buddy.

"Hi Echo," she said when his inquisitive black eyes regarded her from below. No doubt, he'd heard her little moans.

No matter how many times Tarzan scolded her, she could never manage to stay quiet.

Disappointment weighed heavy, as if Echo stood on her heart. She lifted her lips in a bitter smile.

On his haunches in classic gorilla style, the silverback scratched his chest, looking for all the world like an unexcited corporate executive wiling away his boardroom hours in the jungle.

Earlier, there'd been angry shouts; faint in volume, but loud for its foreign sound in the noisy rainforest. Since then, the pirates had been eerily quiet, but the innocent silence could only last so long.

Jane pushed away from the nest's edge and flopped backward on the leaves she and Tarzan had gathered only days before. Desperate to return to a fantasy of Tarzan, she stroked through the moisture between her legs with clinical precision, but the moment had passed. The letdown of not having her grinning, shaggy-haired ape man come home, crushed her horny desire.

Long-necked cranes passed gracefully overhead, winging their way to the island's hot fishing spots. At choke-zone elevation above the large white birds, the tiny speck of a lone jet crossed the blue of another new day.

The modern world, with its fast food drive-thru's and Wi-Fi connections, would never learn of how a primitive man, raised by apes, had turned tragedy into heroism and saved her life.

Nor would anyone care. Not one iota. Not even her *civilized* family, whom she imagined were fighting over the crumbs of her estate this very moment.

Once again, her stomach clenched. Restless hours of constant worry, her begging God to save Tarzan, came delivered up in the form of the dry heaves.

Like a hangover, without the fun of getting drunk.

Jane pitched sideways, curled into a ball, and let the nausea run its course. When the queasiness abated, she rolled to her back and flung a hand over her eyes to block out the morning sun. *Fuck it.* If her nose plugged up, she'd just breathe through her mouth, but morning was her favorite time of day and the tune of a nearby songbird pulled her hand away. Staring up, watching the sky turn fifty shades of pink, she forced herself to consider the possibility her jungle man might not make it home.

If that eventuality came true, it would leave her with a band of gorillas for friends, more coconuts than she could eat, and a remote tropical island on which to survive. The thought left a hollowness inside of her so large—she could safely hide for the rest of her life.

Monkeys screeched *good morning* salutations in the canopy below as they battled for rights over some damn fruit tree.

Jane closed her eyes and inhaled the jungle's perfume carried on the trade wind breeze. Behind the screen of her eyelids, she closed out the world and the misery it brought.

Allowed to wander at will, her mind drifted to the last moments spent in Tarzan's arms. The way his knees pushed to widen the spread of her thighs as he raised the arrowed head of his cock. Jane's breath caught on a sob, remembering the feel of when he slowly pressed his way inside.

Another mental image turned her frown into a smile—he'd have a big surprise in less than a year since her injected birth-control hadn't been renewed.

TARZAN SUCKED IN A breath of much needed air as the last dark-skinned male ran past where he lay hidden in the leaves. He had managed stay one step ahead and avoid being seen, but short of killing them, he hadn't thought of a way to drive them away. Slaying would be a last option, one he would choose if given no choice.

The three males, whose body coverings were covered in dirt, followed a trail leading them further from their boat. Tarzan clenched his fists, stumped on how to force them to leave his jungle island and never come back.

A spotted leopard crept along the footway behind the bad *mans*, eyes and ears pointed forward in its way of hunting. This time, he hoped the cat would do more than play with her food.

After watching the yellow tail twitch out of sight, an idea sprouted. Grinning to himself, Tarzan nodded. Again, the jungle island provided the necessities for life.

When he'd rolled to his feet, he climbed the first available tree to scramble out onto a branch halfway up the sky-high trunk. A thick vine hung in front of his nose in invitation, as if it'd grown without hesitation for his use. After a quick tug-check, he leaned back and took the plunge.

Tarzan wrapped his legs around the vine and held himself in place. The wind whistled past his ears, blowing his hair straight back from his face. Cool morning air invigorated his mind, body, and soul.

Confident of his plan, he gripped the vine with one hand while he cupped the other beside his mouth. *"Ahh-yahyahyah-yah-ahh!"*

Immediately, the reaction of the living jungle responded in a frenzy of screeches and cries. Great flocks of birds flew into the air, turning the sky dark with their numbers. Roars of leopards rose in the air, their throaty calls blended with great silverback apes beating their chests.

Beyond the lowest drop in his swing, Tarzan didn't take his eyes off the thick branch he'd chosen to land on. Up, up, *annnd* release—to land in a crouched position.

He cupped his hands around his mouth. "*Ahh-yahyahyah-yah-ahh!*"

A trumpeted reply from a charging bull elephant blasted moments before the small herd answered his call to action. Trees toppled like thin twigs as the rumbling group crashed through the underbrush and crossed beneath the limb Tarzan stood upon. Soon, the elephants were swallowed up as quickly as they appeared with only the trampling of plants to be heard.

To not lose sight of the stampeding herd, Tarzan ran the length of the tree's bough before he used the thinner, springed end to launch himself out and catch hold of another vine. With his hands gripping tight and his legs swinging free, he flew in a sideways arc to the right, through the trees, and followed his elephant friends.

"*Ooh-ooh!*" Echo breezed past Tarzan riding a vine of his own, thick fur waving in the breezy air. Clearly in his element, the great ape released a single-handed hold to leapfrog off the back of an elephant and vault gracefully onto another vine.

Smaller monkeys leapt through the trees, chattering excitedly.

Tarzan swung up high in the air to land feet first on another wide branch. He paused, breathing heavily, and smiled as the horde of jungle animals gave chase to three humans who appeared to be running for their lives.

"*Cheep.*" The white-faced monkey slid down along a thin stalk of twining ivy to settle itself on Tarzan's shoulder. The spindly cousin of the gorillas babbled to a wave of passing monkeys in the trees, then curled its tail in a choke hold around Tarzan's neck and bobbed up and down to watch the other animals.

The human bad *mans* shouted several times and backed their threats with bangs from the rock-sticks.

Tarzan ventured further out on the branch until a clear view of the vast ocean appeared. Yellow-beaked birds dove like falling rocks from the sky. At the last moment, they would pull up sharply, turn, and dive again. Past where the frothy white water crashed onto the sand, other species of brightly colored birds squawked at ear piercing levels, flapping their wings and pecking the unprotected heads of the screaming *mans.*

Wooden arms of the little boat dug into the water at a rapid rate, the dark-skinned males became a blur of motion.

Elephants lined the sandy beach and trumpeted their challenge to the unwanted visitors.

"*Cheep-cheep,*" the monkey issued a threat of his own as he bounced on Tarzan's shoulder.

A quick slide down a vine and soft sand cushioned his landing. He strode out of the shadowed jungle and into the bright sun and hot beach. With each dig into the water, the boatful of humans moved further away. One of the *mans* lifted his killing stick and leveled it beside his eye. A breeze stretched the puff of smoke before the bang reached Tarzan's ears, and a harmless clump of sand flew up near the water's edge.

The male raised a skinny arm and shouted in his guttural tones toward the shore. If it was a threat he promised, a threat they would get.

Tarzan took a deep breath, then called toward the breaking water, "*Ahh-yahyahyah-yah-ahh!*"

First, one pointed fin broke the water's surface, and then another. Several more joined in as though the pack of meat-eater fish understood only a thin sheet of wood lay between them and their morning breakfast.

For the first time since the sun had set the night before, he took a normal breath of calming air. Together, he and the monkey watched the rowboat grow smaller as it veered toward a larger boat in the distance, the circling fins happy to tag along. Victory for the moment, but how long would it last?

"Jane safe." Tarzan reached up and gave the little guy a friendly scratch. "For now."

Chapter Seven

Four weeks later...

Tarzan scraped Jane's hair away from her face and held the long strands in one hand. His other arm wrapped her hips to keep his female from falling head first over the side of the nest.

"Fuck, I feel like shit," she said, spitting to clear her mouth.

"No." He kissed the back of her neck. "Jane not squishy."

"Hope it's not malar—"

Her body went rigid in his arms, and the heaving began again. Sweat broke out on her body where his skin touched hers. Eyes clamped tightly closed and her face three shades of red, she made a choking sound that nearly stopped his heart. When she coughed and began to breathe again, he let out a gust of breath he'd been holding in.

Two sunrises in a row, Jane had opened her morning eyes in much the same way to scramble for the edge of the nest. His hand trembled as he gently stroked over the mossy-soft skin of her face. The sickness finished for the moment, white lines on her face smoothed as the tension drained out. Heavy lidded, she leaned back against his chest to rest, her body limp, damp, and breathing fast.

"Oh God, Tarzan. What the hell's the matter with me?"

"*Ooh-ooh*." While he had seen spotted cats perform this ritual many times in the jungle, but he himself had never tossed his eaten food. Nor had a gorilla, to the best of his knowledge. "Bad bananas. Jane fine."

"I hope that's all it is. Sure wish I had a toothbrush."

He reached for the scrap of blue cloth she used to rub her teeth to clean them. A small piece from a larger portion that used to be her leg coverings. He handed it to her.

Jane glanced at his offering and grimaced, then pushed his hand away. "Nooo," she moaned. "Get it away from me."

Tarzan looked at the clean cloth, shrugged his confusion, then dropped it over the side of the nest.

"What are you doing?" She leaned away from his chest and sat up to peer over the edge, her beautiful breasts swaying with the motion. "I didn't say to throw it away, just get it out of my face."

Sick one moment, angry the next. What was this sickness? When she turned to glare at him through the crazed eyes of an unreasonable female, he peeled his lips away from his teeth and offered his alpha female a grin of submission with the back of his hand.

"Oh, so you think it's funny, huh? I'm puking my guts out, probably dying from some unknown disease on this god-forsaken island, and you're laughing at me. How can you be so insensiti—" Jane's mouth sounds abruptly stopped and her face turned the color of mashed bugs. The muscles of her tanned stomach jumped twice before she hurled herself to the edge of the nest, barely giving him time to wrap a protective arm around her bare hips.

Garbled noise that sounded painful, accompanied her retching form. The moment passed quickly, and he helped her to lay back on the straw sleeping mat. She closed her eyes and sighed.

His female, his responsibility. She lay sick and he needed to help.

"Tarzan make Jane feel better." Leaning down, he brushed a kiss to her forehead.

"Contrary to popular belief, sex is not the cure all." She opened an eye to peer up at him. "It ain't happening, Jungle-boy, so don't even think about it."

After her eye closed, he sat back and licked his lips. A frown grew as he tried to understand her long words. He had come a long way in their communication, learning many of her mouth sounds, but when Jane spoke too fast or used words he did not know, an unsettled feeling crept in. If he didn't know better, he might even think it was fear.

"Sex," he repeated, because that was a familiar word. He thought of a couple others. "Think about."

Jane tsked, then rolled away from him to stretch onto her side and moan. The graceful line of her spine flexed as she shifted for a more comfortable position. "Take a hike. Nothing to think about."

In her weakened condition, she wouldn't get far on a jungle walk. He opened his mouth to suggest she sleep, but she cut him off.

"Don't say another word. If you want to help, get me something to drink. I'd love a 7-Up."

Drink, love. His female was thirsty and hungry...again. Tarzan knew exactly what to do and where to find what she needed.

Quietly, so as not to ruffle Jane's bad mood, he crossed the nest and chose the vine that would swing him toward the sheltered area near the flowing waters. Two vines later, he dropped to the ground and searched for the plant with long pink flowers and tough scaly roots.

Years ago, when he suffered from a terrible stomach ache, Tarzan's ape mother gathered this root for him to eat. The pleasant, spicy taste fought his gut pains and he had felt better almost immediately. Spying the plant, he dug under the soil to break off a small portion, then went to fill an empty gourd with water before returning home.

Other than to roll onto her back, Jane hadn't moved. One arm was thrown over her eyes, the other lightly rubbed her stomach.

Tarzan knelt beside her and felt relieved when no sweat glistened across her breasts. Her nipples, a darker color as of late, lay soft, inviting, teasing his lips to taste the coral tips.

His thickened male part would have to wait.

Using his knife, he shaved a thin piece of root. "Jane, open."

She cracked open her lids and smiled up at him, then crossed her eyes to focus on the knife hovering just above her lips. "What are you doing?"

"Open."

"What is it?"

He sighed. His female, always with the mouth sounds. "Nice food for happy gut."

"Happy gut, huh?" By her pinched frown, she didn't look like she believed him, and wiggled to sit up. "I'm all for a happy *anything* right now."

Her eyes never left his face as he carefully placed the sliver of root on her tongue.

She chewed, her brows first dipping down then shot straight up. "It's ginger!" Smiling, she opened her mouth for the next thin slice.

He handed her the water gourd and watched with satisfaction when she drank the contents dry.

"You always know what I need, don't you?"

"Tarzan help Jane."

A mischievous grin lifted her lips. "I've got something else with needs."

His female was feeling much better.

TARZAN'S BACK MUSCLES jumped in response to the blood-pumping slide of Jane's soft hands. With his impatient morning-tool driven deep inside her damp warmth, memories of the bad *mans* who had threatened his female dissolved like the occasional ground-clouds that snaked low through the jungle floor.

"*Ooh-ooh.*" He growled, pumping into her willing body. Tightening his butt when pushing forward, exhaling through his mouth when pulling back.

Flowery scents of his aroused mate surrounded their moon bed and filled his mind with all things happy and bright. The normal storm of croaking toads and daybreak's calling birds faded away on the sigh of Jane's soft moans.

Whisper now, scream later. Tarzan grinned and doubled his hip-driving effort.

The miracle of his brave little female who survived the dangerous *pie-rats*, escaped a sinking boat, then washed ashore on his island of all places. He had no mouth sounds for what filled his heart, only a strange burn of watered eyes that warmed him from the inside out whenever he gazed on her beautiful face.

Jane's fingers drifted down from his shoulders in a lazy side-to side caress to fill her palms with his flexing ass. Her nails scratched as she gripped, stoking his raging jungle fire as he thoroughly mated her. Thoughts of her hands moving with his mating motion, feeling the strength of his male part as he rammed inside her, drove him to thrust faster.

Tarzan imagined what she might think of his up, down, bump, and grind. He wanted her female body to move past its basic need of his hardened male tool.

He wanted *proof* of their mating.

A small sliver of his brain—the only part still working—wondered why she had yet to grow fat with his infant. As he rocked into Jane, murmuring *ooh-ooh's* to the sound of her *oh god's*, his stimulated mind worked on ways to grow that particular fruit.

Love.

His hair slid forward like a waterfall to block out the jungle as he lifted to lean his weight onto one arm, then used his free hand to push the hair out of her eyes and palm her sweet face. Beautiful blue eyes, glazed with stark desire, peered back at him with half-closed lids. The growing flush on her neck and plump breasts deepened the warmth he held for his female.

A warm but aching pressure puffed his chest from the inside out.

Could this be the *love* Jane spoke of? He wasn't hungry, but she satisfied a ravenous craving within him.

Under the muscles of his chest, his heart quickened, matching the rhythm set by his mating tool. Nature and the compelling drive to breed controlled his actions. He slid his hand across the front of Jane's neck, wrapping his palm over her throat, pleased when she tilted back her head.

Submission. Complete trust.

Tremendous need for his mate broke over his body in a fine sheen. The impatient longing slammed into his hardened sex. Jane's long legs curled around his hips and she dug her heels into his back. The familiar tingle started at the base of his spine. His balls drew tight.

Tarzan caressed his way down to cup her soft breast. The weight in his palm felt heavier, the size larger, but when she moaned and thrust her hips, he tossed his thoughts aside and gently pinched her rosy nipple. Fascinated, he pulled, and felt her answering squeeze on his male part below. He kept thrusting, sliding into her wetness in the way of jungle mating. Her other nipple looked lonely, so he switched sides to stroke and pull some more.

Jane's eyes shut tight, as a look of agony crossed her features. "Tarzan...I can barely breathe."

Shocked he had somehow injured his squirming female, he froze and placed his palm over the rabbit-quick beat of her heart. "Jane hurt?"

Beneath him, she stilled, then pushed his shoulder to roll and reverse their position. Her moist, hot core cocooned his tool. A huge smile stretched the corners of her mouth, and her fawn-brown hair, lifted by the breeze, floated over her shoulders to tumble down her back.

"Not hardly," Jane replied, her mouth tones sounding rough. Bending low, she brushed her lips across his throat and ground her damp female center into him. "I meant, you have me so turned-on, who needs air?"

The mind-numbing drag and slide on his male part as she glided up and drifted down, staggered each breath released from his lungs.

"Tarzan...understand," the admission left his mouth, followed by a hard pulse from his tool. He gripped her rounded hips, guiding her. Pumped upward between her widespread thighs and watched the veins of his glistening sex disappear in and out. He kept her moving in the special way that rolled his eyeballs to the back of his head.

When she leaned forward to seize his lips, he took his time touching their tongues and enjoying her taste completely. He sucked her lower lip into his mouth, only releasing when she straightened to sit up and ride him harder. Her head arched back, hair and tits bouncing as she raced to the place when their bodies clenched and breathing became ragged. An emotion welled inside of him, clogging his throat.

One day, Jane would bear Tarzan young ones. He tenderly caressed her stomach with the hopeful thought. Many babies, if possible. The loneliness in his past as the only human on the jungle island would soon be nothing more than a distant memory.

"I'm gonna...." Jane cried out, her female channel tightened. "I love you, Tarzan."

"Tarzan love Jane," he gasped, arching his back as he drove his mating tool deep within his female's body to reach his favorite peak.

In the jungle beyond their nest, the huffing of apes went wild. Monkeys shrieked as the thumping of solid chests beat in the background. Gorillas called their acknowledgement of the rising passion between their alpha male and his mated female.

Two thoughts swirled in Tarzan's love crazed mind as he cried out and spilled his essence: *Forever. My Jane.*

Don't miss out!

Visit the website below and you can sign up to receive emails whenever Sheri Fredricks publishes a new book. There's no charge and no obligation.

https://books2read.com/r/B-A-WCJH-YWXX

BOOKS 2 READ

Connecting independent readers to independent writers.

Did you love *Forever My Jane*? Then you should read *Esme, Door 1*[1] by Sheri Fredricks!

[2]

Desperate times call for deliciously wicked measures...

With only ten dollars to her name and a mortgage looming, Esme is out of options. She's followed all the rules, but when a mysterious *Help Wanted* ad promises quick cash, her curiosity—and desperation—wins out. What she doesn't expect is an automated interview... and a job offer with wildly unconventional terms.

Faced with a choice between losing everything or stepping into a new reality that challenges her limits, Esme must decide:

---

1. https://books2read.com/u/mgLXgq

2. https://books2read.com/u/mgLXgq

walk away or take a leap of faith. What begins as survival quickly spirals into an erotic journey that awakens her confidence, challenges her boundaries, and sets her on a path of sensual discovery.

ESME is a bold, provocative erotic romance that blends real-world stakes with sizzling fantasy. Perfect for fans of steamy stories featuring strong, relatable heroines, unexpected twists, and red-hot encounters that push the limits. If you love tales of temptation, empowerment, and the thrill of the forbidden, you'll fall hard for Esme.

Read more at https://www.sherifredricks.com.

About the Author

Sheri Fredricks grew up on the central coast of California and resides within minutes of the pristine sunny beaches. She's a Border Collie fan, loves to eat sushi, and is addicted to Facebook. A writer of romance, she's the award-winning author of the shapeshifting Centaurs Series, Jungle Island Series, Monica Beggs, and many more. Sheri is currently writing more steamy, sexy stories for her voracious fans.

Read more at https://www.sherifredricks.com.